The Letter

Written by: Hannah Evans
Illustrated by: Erika Grimm

Dedicated to each person who was deliberately put in my path by God's grace.

Explore www.anniesadventures.org & www.curiouskid.org for additional activities.

Dear sweet Annie,
I miss you so much! If I could, I would fly us to exotic places and go exploring — like crawling through the pyramids in Egypt. I would in a heartbeat.

I loved our adventures together and your wild sense of imagination. You said our car could travel through time and space.

Even though we couldn't stop everywhere, we imagined what life was like back when the old towns were busy, vibrant, and alive.

You said every state we stopped in was like going to a foreign land.

Please know that
I think about you
each and every day.

I am sick, and my sickness cannot be fixed with medicine alone...

Every day is like
an epic battle ...

... and sometimes the bad guys are bigger and stronger than me.

But then I look at your photo, Annie, and I grow stronger.

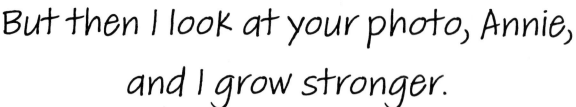

Never feel guilty or that you are to blame for my addiction, because

you are the reason
that I keep trying and growing stronger.

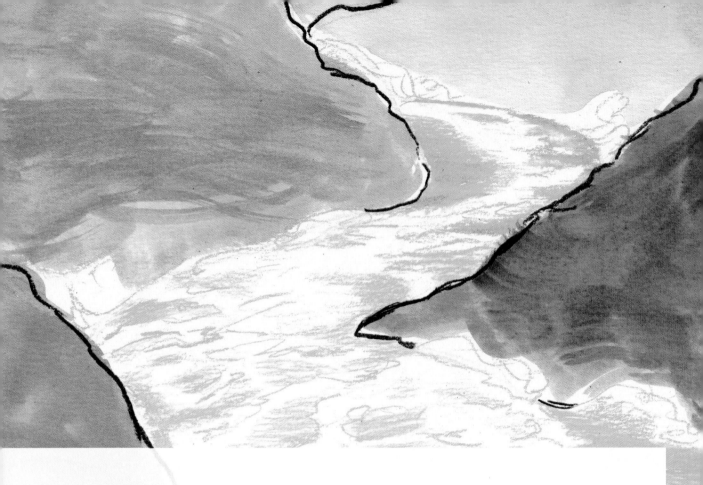

When the drugs enter my body,
it's like rivers of water
flowing through deep canyons,
twisting and turning.

It's all I can think about and
all I can feel.

Also, know in your heart
that you are special; there is
no one in the world like you.

You have lots of awesome adventures ahead of you. I will try to join you soon. Annie, I may not return and be the "perfect" mom you deserve yet. There is power in the word "yet," and I am working hard to overcome this, for you.

Love, Mom

Mawmaw explains, "Annie, I know it hurts you, and it is okay to cry, but remember that she loves you, and I love you. This illness your mom is facing is not something to be ashamed of or to think less of yourself over. This has changed you, Annie. You will be a fighter. You may not feel like it now, but you will be stronger than others."

Sometimes, it is hard for us to talk about how we feel. Sometimes, our feelings can be overwhelming, which means they are too big or too much for us. One way to explain how we feel is to write a letter to someone. If you are sad, sit down and write a letter to anyone, at any time. It is your choice to give the person the letter, but it will make you feel better.

Dear _____,

_____

_____

_____

_____

_____

_____

Sincerely,

_____

Author:
Hannah Evans

Hannah Evans, formerly Gearhart, was raised in Fayette County, Pennsylvania. Her family resides on Chestnut Ridge, nestled in the Appalachian Mountains. Hannah is a graduate of Penn State University, where she earned a Bachelor's degree in Business. Additionally, she earned her Master's in Education from West Virginia University. The first five years of her teaching profession were in West Virginia at Gilmer County High School and Richwood High School. The following five years were in Pennsylvania— at Chambersburg Senior High School and, currently, at New Oxford Middle School. Inspired by her grandmother's love of genealogy, Hannah has taught history and the social sciences. From her life experiences, she understands the hardships of poverty and the struggles of being raised in Appalachia. As a teacher, she noticed the unique challenges and emotional hardships faced by her students. Hannah created Annie's Appalachian Adventures to help mend broken hearts with the hopes that all children can love themselves and achieve their dreams.